March Mischief

The kitchen clock said seven-thirty. The sun was starting to shine through the window over the sink. Bradley smiled.

He didn't see any doughnuts, but he poured himself a glass of juice. He drank it and listened to a few birds outside the window. Then he remembered the leprechaun statue on the porch. He wanted to check it out again before the contest the next day.

Bradley opened the front door. He stepped onto the porch in his bare feet.

Then he gasped.

The leprechaun was gone!

Calendar Mysteries
March Mischief

by **Ron Roy**

illustrated by
John Steven Gurney

A STEPPING STONE BOOK™

Random House 🏠 New York

This book is dedicated to teachers.
—R.R.

To my nephew, Joey O!
—J.S.G.

Text copyright © 2010 by Ron Roy
Illustrations and map copyright © 2010 by John Steven Gurney

Visit us on the Web!
www.ronroy.com
www.randomhouse.com/kids

Educators and librarians, for a variety of teaching tools, visit us at
www.randomhouse.com/teachers

Library of Congress Cataloging-in-Publication Data
Roy, Ron.
March mischief / by Ron Roy ; illustrated by John Steven Gurney. — 1st ed.
    p.   cm. — (Calendar mysteries) "A Stepping Stone Book."
Summary: When three leprechaun statues disappear right before St. Patrick's Day, Bradley, Brian, Nate, Lucy, and other friends follow clues in order to prove that Lucky O'Leary is innocent of the crime.
ISBN 978-0-375-85663-1 (trade) — ISBN 978-0-375-95663-8 (lib. bdg.)
[1. Mystery and detective stories. 2. Statues—Fiction. 3. Lost and found possessions—Fiction. 4. Saint Patrick's Day—Fiction. 5. Twins—Fiction. 6. Brothers and sisters—Fiction. 7. Cousins—Fiction.]
I. Gurney, John Steven, ill. II. Title.
PZ7.R8139Mar 2010   [Fic]—dc22   2009006110

Printed in the United States of America

10 9 8 7 6 5 4 3 2 1

First Edition

Contents

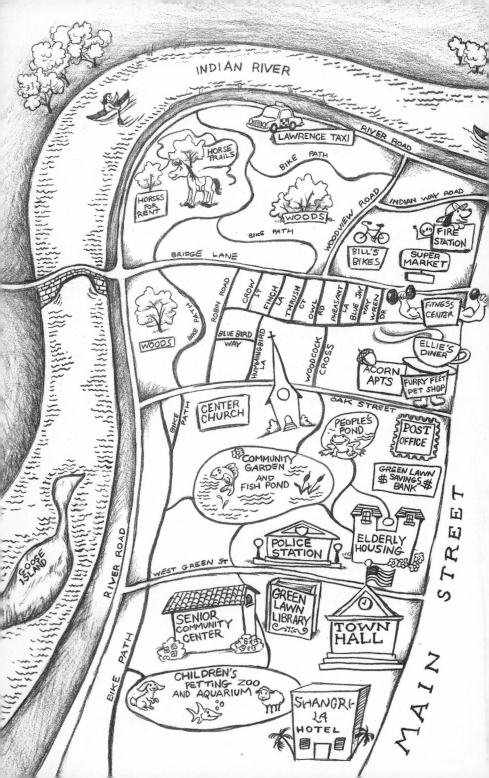

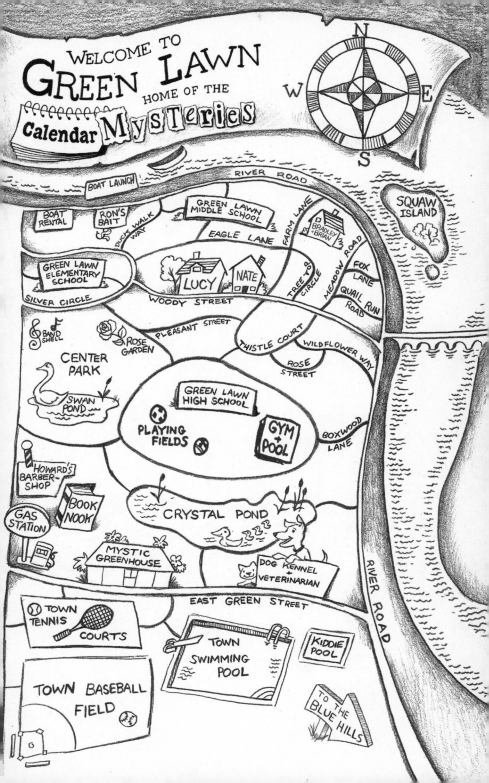

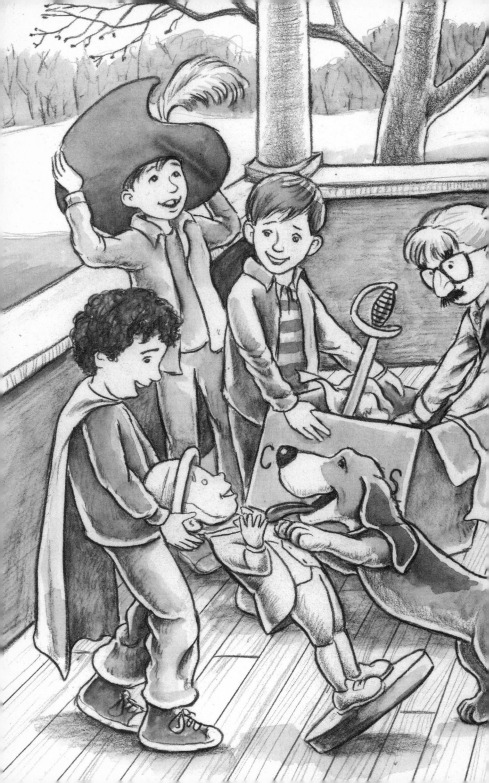

1
A Leprechaun Named Pal

"Batman!" shouted Nate.

"A pirate!" yelled Brian.

"Groucho!" cried Lucy.

It was Friday, March 15. In two days it would be St. Patrick's Day. Every year people in Green Lawn had a St. Patrick's Day contest. They dressed leprechaun statues in funny outfits. The mayor chose a winner, and there was a prize.

Everyone who entered the contest bought a leprechaun statue for five dollars. The money went to help a local food bank.

The four kids had chipped in and bought their statue together. They were on Bradley and Brian's front porch with a cardboard box of costumes. The kids were trying costumes on the leprechaun and on themselves.

Lucy was in first grade with the three boys. She was staying with her cousin, Dink Duncan, for a year. Her parents were in Arizona helping to build a school on a reservation.

Nate Hathaway and his big sister, Ruth Rose, lived next door to Dink on Woody Street.

Bradley and Brian Pinto were twins and lived with their parents and older brother, Josh, on Farm Lane.

Pal, the Pintos' dog, sniffed the green leprechaun statue. It stood about two feet tall. The statue looked like a little

green man with a bow tie. Its face had
plump green cheeks and a green beard.
Green buckled shoes were on its feet.

Pal licked the leprechaun's face.

"Hey, that gives me another idea!"
Bradley said. "Why don't we dress the
statue as Pal?"

"Huh?" Nate said. "A leprechaun
dog?"

"Sure, why not?" Bradley asked.
"Everyone else will make theirs some
sports hero or comic book guy. We'd be
the only ones with a dog!"

"Can we do that?" Brian asked.

"Why not?" Bradley asked. "The
mayor's rules didn't say it had to be
human!"

"That's a great idea!" Lucy said. "We
can make floppy ears, a tail, and a doggy
nose! And we can name it Pal."

Bradley pulled off the hat he'd been
trying on and ran inside. A minute later

he came back with a box of art supplies. Bradley took out scissors, glue, clay, markers, and construction paper.

The kids spent the rest of the afternoon changing the leprechaun into a basset hound.

Lucy made floppy ears. They looked just like Pal's ears.

Nate molded some brown clay into a nose.

Brian used a tube sock for the tail. He made brown marks on it, like the ones on Pal's tail.

"It doesn't look like a dog," Brian said. "He needs fur."

"I have an idea," Bradley said. He went in the kitchen to Pal's bed. Pal liked to sleep on one of Bradley's old brown sweaters. Bradley grabbed the sweater and took it outside.

"What're you doing?" Brian asked.

"You'll see," Bradley said. He cut the

sweater's sleeves off. Then he pulled it over the leprechaun's head. The sweater made the leprechaun look furry. Sort of.

"He looks good," Lucy said.

"He smells bad," Brian said.

Bradley put his nose next to the leprechaun. "It's the sweater," he said.

"Well, if the mayor picks the smelliest statue, we should win," Nate said.

Pal barked at the leprechaun. He rubbed his nose against the sweater. Then he curled up near its green feet and went to sleep.

2
Lost
Leprechaun

Bradley woke up thirsty the next morning. He knew there was a carton of orange juice in the fridge. His stomach growled. Maybe he'd find doughnuts in the kitchen, too.

He looked over at his brother's bed. Brian was sound asleep.

Bradley slipped out of the room. He tiptoed down the hallway and stairs so he wouldn't wake his family.

The kitchen clock said seven-thirty.

The sun was starting to shine through the window over the sink. Bradley smiled.

He didn't see any doughnuts, but he poured himself a glass of juice. He drank it and listened to a few birds outside the window. Then he remembered the leprechaun statue on the porch. He wanted to check it out again before the contest the next day.

Bradley opened the front door. He stepped onto the porch in his bare feet.

Then he gasped.

The leprechaun was gone!

Bradley turned and ran back inside the house. He bumped into Josh in his pajamas.

"Whoa, slow down! What's the matter?" Josh said.

"The leprechaun is gone!" Bradley shouted just as his parents came into the kitchen.

"What's wrong?" his mother asked. "Why the shouting?"

"The leprechaun ran away from home," Josh said, cracking a grin.

Bradley raced up the stairs to his room. "Get up, Brian!" he shouted. He yanked off his pajamas and started getting dressed.

"What's all the yelling?" Brian asked. One of his eyes peeked out from under the bedcovers.

"The leprechaun is gone!" Bradley said.

Brian sat up. His hair was all spiky. "What do you mean?" he asked.

"Bri, it's not on the porch where we left it!" Bradley said. "Someone must have stolen it."

Brian yawned. "Who'd want a smelly old leprechaun?" he asked.

Bradley tossed a pillow at his brother. "I want it!" he said.

Brian ducked from the pillow. "What are you gonna do?" he asked.

"Look for it," Bradley said. He pulled on his sneakers. "And you're gonna help."

Two minutes later Bradley and Brian were in the backyard.

"Brad, if someone stole it, why are we searching our own yard?" Brian asked.

Bradley peered inside a clump of bushes. "Maybe someone hid it out here to play a trick on us."

The brothers looked under shrubs, in the barn, and even up in trees.

Their mother opened the back door. "You boys come in and eat some breakfast!" she yelled.

Bradley and Brian walked back into the kitchen. Before sitting down at the table, Bradley called Lucy. "Someone stole the leprechaun!" he told her. "Call Nate and come over."

"Maybe someone just took it for a joke," the boys' mother said after Bradley hung up. She looked at Josh.

"Don't look at me!" he said. "It's probably your buddy Nate. He loves playing jokes on people."

Bradley thought about Nate. Would he steal the leprechaun they had all worked on so hard?

While they were eating oatmeal, the phone rang. Josh jumped for it.

"Hello?" he said. "Just a minute."

Josh placed the phone next to Bradley's orange juice. "For you," he said. "Someone with a bad cold."

Bradley picked up the phone and said, "Hello?"

"Lucky O'Leary stole your leprechaun," a hoarse voice said.

Then the caller hung up.

3
The Big
Blue House

Bradley stared at the phone.

"Who was that?" his mother asked.

"I don't know," Bradley said. "But whoever it was said Lucky O'Leary took our leprechaun."

"Lucky?" said the boys' mother. "That's absurd. He's such a nice boy."

"It can't be Lucky," Josh said. "He's away at college."

"He comes home for weekends sometimes," Brian said.

Just then someone knocked on the door. Bradley let Nate and Lucy in.

They sat at the table while Bradley told them about the phone call.

"Who is Lucky O'Leary?" Lucy asked.

"He's this college kid we know," Josh said. "Trust me, he'd never steal anything."

"And he's rich!" Nate said. "Dink, Josh, and Ruth Rose helped him find a million-dollar lottery ticket!"

"Wow!" Lucy said. "And you don't know who called you?"

Bradley shook his head. "He had a hoarse voice, though," he said.

"Could it have been a girl?" Lucy asked.

Bradley shrugged. He tried to remember the voice. "It was so hoarse I couldn't tell. It could have been a girl, I guess," he said.

Bradley took the last bite of his

oatmeal. "Come on, let's go to Lucky's house."

"What are we gonna say to him?" Brian asked. "We can't just accuse him."

"I won't," Bradley said. "I'll tell him about the phone call."

The kids all wore sweaters. The day was windy but not too cold. Pal was on his leash. He trotted along happily, sniffing the ground.

"Where does Lucky live?" Lucy asked as they cut through the school playground.

"On Robin Road," Nate said. "He's got about a hundred brothers and sisters. And every one of them has red hair!"

The kids hiked down Main Street. They took a right on Bridge Lane, next to the fitness center.

When they came to Robin Road, Bradley pointed. "That's where Lucky lives."

It was a big blue house. The front yard was covered with bikes, balls, and other toys. Three boys with red hair were kicking a soccer ball.

A short girl with red hair was sitting on the porch steps. A leprechaun statue stood next to her. It was exactly like Bradley's statue, except it wore a dress, a blond wig, and lipstick. Cardboard wings were glued to its back. The wings were shiny with silver glitter.

"Don't look!" the girl yelled when she saw Pal and the kids. She stood up to block her fairy-princess leprechaun.

The kids walked toward the blue house.

"Hey, guys!" one of the redheaded boys shouted.

Bradley let Pal off his leash. Pal trotted over to a red wagon and began sniffing.

"Is your brother Lucky home?" Bradley asked.

"He's in the house," the girl said. Her face was all freckles and a big smile. She walked over to pet Pal.

"He came home from college for the leprechaun contest," one of her brothers said.

Nate nudged Bradley on the arm.

Just then the door opened. A tall guy with red hair stepped onto the porch. He looked at all the kids. Then he glanced at his watch.

"Hi, Lucky," Bradley said. All of a sudden he felt foolish. Was it possible that Lucky would steal a silly leprechaun? But what about that phone call?

"Yo, Bradley, or is it Brian?" Lucky said.

"Bradley," he said. "Um, I got a phone call this morning, and—"

Suddenly they all heard a siren. Seconds later a police cruiser turned the corner and parked in front of the blue house. Two police officers got out.

4
Mischief

Bradley recognized Officer Fallon and Officer Keene.

Bradley's mouth fell open. Pal barked at all the excitement. All the kids stopped playing. The little girl hugged one of her dolls.

"Hi, kids," Officer Fallon said. He smiled under his floppy mustache. "Hello, Lucky. How's school?"

"School is cool," Lucky said.

A woman with red hair came out

onto the porch behind Lucky. Two of his redheaded brothers stepped out after her. Bradley knew they went to the same school, but he didn't know their names.

"Hello, Roberta," Officer Fallon said.

"Hello, Officer Fallon," Mrs. O'Leary answered. "What brings you our way?"

"I'm afraid there's been some mischief in town, Roberta," Officer Fallon said. "Someone's been stealing leprechauns."

"Ours got stolen, too!" Bradley said. "Right off our porch!"

"Huh," Officer Fallon said. "That makes three so far, then. Mr. Paskey at the Book Nook said his was taken last night. He left it out for the paint to dry. And Mrs. Wong at the pet shop says hers got swiped off her deck."

"But what does that have to do with us?" Roberta O'Leary asked. "We still have Josephine's leprechaun." She pointed to the fairy-princess leprechaun on their porch steps.

Officer Fallon gave Lucky a strange look. "I'm arresting Lucky for the thefts." He and his partner walked toward the porch. Officer Keene was holding handcuffs.

Bradley couldn't believe what he was seeing. Lucky O'Leary was no thief. He tutored high school kids who needed extra help. He was a volunteer fireman. He'd never go around stealing leprechauns!

"I didn't steal anything!" Lucky said. He took a step backward.

"My son is innocent!" Roberta O'Leary said.

"That's not what we heard," Officer Fallon said. He took Lucky by the arm. "Come with us to the station, son."

Lucky's little sister Josephine began to cry. "He didn't do anything!" she said.

"You leave my brother alone!"

The officers put Lucky in the cruiser's backseat.

All the redheads charged up onto the porch. "Mommy! What's happening?" they all asked.

"Everything will be fine," Mrs. O'Leary said. Then she herded her gang into the house.

Bradley couldn't move. He felt like a statue.

5
Lucky's
Unlucky Day

The cruiser took off. All the O'Learys were in the house. The yard was quiet. The fairy-princess leprechaun stood all alone on the porch.

"Boy, that was weird," Nate said.

The kids and Pal started walking toward Main Street.

"Do you think Lucky really took the leprechauns?" Lucy asked.

"No. Lucky is honest," Brian said.

"But someone must think he did it,"

Bradley said. "Someone called the cops on him."

"Maybe Mrs. Wong or Mr. Paskey saw Lucky do it," Nate said.

"I'd bet anything he didn't steal them!" Bradley said. "This has to be a big mistake."

"I feel bad for Lucky," Lucy said. "But how can we get our leprechaun back? The contest is tomorrow morning!"

"We'll figure something out," Bradley said. "If we can find the real thief, Lucky will get out of jail. And we'll get our leprechaun."

When the kids and Pal reached the twins' house, they got a surprise.

Two beat-up bikes leaned against the porch. Two of Lucky's brothers were sitting on the steps. They stood up.

"Hey," Bradley said. "How'd you get here before us?"

"We took River Road," one of the

boys said. "I'm Ben, and this is Ralphie. We have something to tell you."

All six kids sat on the porch. Pal found a tennis ball to chew on.

"Sorry about Lucky," Brian said.

"That's why we're here," Ben said. "Lucky didn't take your leprechaun. We did. We took the others, too."

"We called you this morning and blamed it on Lucky," Ralphie said.

"But why?" asked Bradley.

"We were mad at Lucky," Ben said. "He got Mom to punish us for messing around in his room. So we came up with an idea. We stole the three statues last night. We dragged them home in our sister's wagon. Then we hid them in Lucky's closet, under his gym clothes."

"Then we called you," Ralphie said. "We just wanted to mess with Lucky, not get him arrested!"

"Anyway," Ben went on, "after Officer Fallon took Lucky away, we ran upstairs to his bedroom. We figured we'd bring the three leprechauns to Officer Fallon and tell him the truth."

Ben and Ralphie glanced at each other.

"So, what happened?" Nate asked.

"When we looked in the closet, the leprechauns were gone," Ben said.

Bradley thought Ben O'Leary was going to cry.

6
Everyone
Loves Lucky

"Someone swiped them again?" Nate asked.

"We don't know what to do!" Ben said. "Our mom is upset, Lucky is in jail, and everyone's crying all over the house!"

"You really should tell Officer Fallon that you did it," Lucy said.

"We want to!" Ralphie said. "But the leprechauns are gone. How can we explain that?"

"There's something I don't under-
stand," Bradley said. "How could Mrs.
Wong or Mr. Paskey report that Lucky
stole their leprechauns when he didn't
do it? You guys took them."

"I don't get that, either," Ben said.

"Maybe Mrs. Wong or Mr. Paskey
saw one of you and thought you were
your big brother," Nate suggested. "You
sort of all look alike."

"Let's go ask them," Brian said.

"Good idea!" Bradley said. He put
Pal in the house.

"Why can't we bring Pal?" asked Lucy.

"Because he'll bark at all the pets in
Mrs. Wong's shop," Bradley explained.

The kids headed down Eagle Lane.
They cut through Center Park and
crossed Main Street in front of the Furry
Feet Pet Shop. A bell tinkled when
they opened the door. Mrs. Wong was
cleaning a tropical fish tank.

A box of bunny rabbits stood on a table. Parakeets and canaries sang from a row of cages.

"Hi, kids," said Mrs. Wong. She wiped her hands on a cloth. "How can I help you today?"

"We heard about your stolen leprechaun," Brian said. "Ours got taken, too!"

"No!" Mrs. Wong said.

"And Officer Fallon told us Mr. Paskey's disappeared, too!" Nate said.

"Goodness!" Mrs. Wong said. "Green Lawn has a leprechaun thief!"

"Officer Fallon thinks it's my brother Lucky," Ben O'Leary said.

Mrs. Wong laughed. "Lucky wouldn't steal a penny!" she said. "He's the most honest kid I know."

Bradley felt even more confused. "You mean you didn't tell Officer Fallon you thought Lucky took your leprechaun?"

"Heavens no," Mrs. Wong said. "I simply told him someone had taken it. I didn't name any names. I have no idea who took my leprechaun."

"Um, it was us, Mrs. Wong," Ralphie admitted. "Ben and I took yours and two others to play a trick on Lucky. We're really sorry." Then they explained how they hid the statues in Lucky's closet, only to find them missing later. "But we'll get yours back before the contest, honest!"

Mrs. Wong grinned. "I accept your apology," she said. "But this whole thing is very strange. Let me know what happens."

"Thanks, Mrs. Wong," Bradley said. "Now we're going to talk to Mr. Paskey."

The bell tinkled again as the six kids left.

They crossed Main Street and passed Howard's Barbershop. They all waved to Howard. He was cutting the mayor's hair.

The kids walked up the steps to the Book Nook. Mr. Paskey was on a ladder, dusting a row of books. "Hello, young readers!" he said.

"Hi, Mr. Paskey!" all six kids said.

The bookseller stepped down from the ladder. "What can I do for you today?" he asked.

"We heard that your leprechaun got stolen," Nate said.

"It did indeed!" Mr. Paskey said. "One moment it was on my sidewalk, and the next, it was gone!"

"Mrs. Wong's got swiped, too," Bradley said.

"And ours, too!" Brian said.

"It's a real-life mystery," Mr. Paskey said. "Who would steal leprechauns right before the contest?"

"We did. My brother and I took them all," Ben said. He and Ralphie blushed as red as Mr. Paskey's bow tie. They explained about the trick they were trying to play on Lucky. They told him how Lucky had gotten arrested.

"Lucky arrested? What utter nonsense!" Mr. Paskey said. "I know Lucky. He worked here part-time a few summers ago. I saw him pick up a nickel off the floor one day. Instead of slipping it in his pocket, he gave it to me. Lucky would never steal leprechauns!"

"You mean you didn't tell Officer Fallon you thought it was Lucky?" Bradley asked.

Mr. Paskey shook his head. "Never."

Bradley looked at the other kids. He knew they were all thinking the same thing he was thinking: none of them had told Officer Fallon that Lucky was the thief. Mrs. Wong hadn't, either. Nor had Mr. Paskey.

So if no one was blaming Lucky, why had Officer Fallon arrested him?

7
Officer
Fallon's Trade

The kids thanked Mr. Paskey. As they were leaving, he said, "Happy reading!"

"This is a mess," Ben said. "Nobody thinks Lucky stole those dumb leprechauns, but he's still in jail."

Bradley could see the police station across Main Street. "Let's go talk to Officer Fallon," he said. "Tell him what you told us. Maybe he'll believe you if we go with you."

The six kids crossed the street to the police station.

Inside, they walked down a quiet hallway. They passed a room where two officers were dressing a leprechaun statue in a tiny police suit.

Officer Fallon was at his desk sipping tea when the kids walked in. "Hello, gang," he said. "What brings you here?"

"We came to see Lucky," Ben said. "Is he okay?"

"Your brother is very comfortable," Officer Fallon said.

"We want to confess!" Ralphie said.

Officer Fallon raised his bushy eyebrows. "What do you mean, Ralphie?"

"We did it. Ben and me." Ralphie and Ben told Officer Fallon how they had stolen all three leprechauns the night before.

"We hid them in Lucky's closet," Ben said.

"We were gonna return them, honest!" Ralphie cried.

"We did it to get back at Lucky," Ben went on. "We were mad at him, so we lied and told Bradley that it was Lucky. And we're really sorry!"

Everyone got quiet.

Bradley could feel his heart beating too fast. "Officer Fallon, who told you that Lucky stole the leprechauns?" he asked. "We talked to Mrs. Wong and Mr. Paskey, and they said they didn't tell you."

Officer Fallon looked at Bradley. He tugged on an earlobe. He smoothed his mustache. "I'm afraid I can't tell you," he finally answered. "Not while an investigation is going on."

Officer Fallon stood up. "Ben and Ralphie, you're very brave to admit what you did," he said. "Now just go get the statues and return them to their owners. Then I'll let Lucky out of jail."

"But that's the problem," Ben said. "The leprechauns aren't in the closet anymore."

"Well, where are they?" Officer Fallon asked.

"We don't know!" Ralphie wailed.

Bradley thought the poor kid was going to burst into tears.

Officer Fallon looked down at the O'Leary brothers. "You don't know where the leprechauns are?"

"No," Ben mumbled.

"Someone stole them from Lucky's closet!" Ralphie said.

"Oh, now I see," Officer Fallon said. "First you stole them, then you hid them, then someone else stole them, right?"

"Right!" Ben and Ralphie both said.

"Some stranger walked into your house and took three leprechauns from Lucky's closet?" Officer Fallon asked.

Ben and Ralphie nodded.

"Well, we have a problem," Officer Fallon said. "I can't let Lucky out of jail until the stolen goods are returned."

"But—but we don't know where they are," Ralphie stuttered.

Officer Fallon sighed. "Sorry, kids, that's the way it will have to be. We'll make a trade. When you give me the leprechauns, I'll give you Lucky."

8
Where
Is Pal?

The kids left the police station. No one knew what to say.

Ben and Ralphie wanted their brother back.

Bradley, Brian, Lucy, and Nate wanted their leprechaun back.

At the fitness center window, they watched two women dressing a leprechaun statue in gym clothes.

"We'd better get home," Ralphie said.

"Don't worry, we'll figure something out," Bradley said.

"See you guys," Ben muttered. He and Ralphie trudged toward Robin Road.

Bradley, Brian, Lucy, and Nate went to the twins' house.

Bradley found a note from his mother:

Gone shopping. Josh is in charge.
Pal seems lonely. Play with him!
Lunch is in the fridge.
                        —Mom

"Where is Pal?" Lucy asked.

Bradley whistled. Pal didn't come.

Brian clapped his hands. Pal still didn't come. "Geez, don't tell me somebody stole him, too!" Brian said.

"Let's go look," Nate said.

The four kids split up and searched the house.

Bradley checked the bedrooms. Josh

was on his bed reading and eating a sandwich.

"Have you seen Pal?" Bradley asked.

"He was in the kitchen when I made my sandwich," Josh said.

"He's not there now," Bradley said. Next, he went to the bedroom he shared with Brian. Pal's tail was sticking out from under Brian's bed.

"There you are," Bradley muttered. He flopped down on the floor next to the bed. "Hi, Pal. Come on out."

Pal didn't move.

"I'll give you a cookie," Bradley said.

Pal wasn't interested.

"Are you mad at me?" Bradley asked.

Pal didn't make a sound.

Bradley peeked under the bed. Pal's big brown eyes looked back at him.

"What have you got there?" Bradley asked. Pal was lying on something brown and fuzzy.

Bradley pulled out the two sleeves he'd cut off his old sweater.

"You miss your sweater?" Bradley asked. "Is that why you're mad? I had to use the sweater for the leprechaun."

Just then the other kids walked in.

"I found him," Bradley said. He showed them the two sweater sleeves. "Pal's mad because we took his old sweater."

Brian, Lucy, and Nate got down on the floor. They all looked under the bed. Pal looked back at them.

"I have an idea," Lucy said.

"He'll come out when he gets hungry," Brian said.

"No, I mean about finding the leprechaun," Lucy said. "Maybe Pal can find it for us!"

The other three just looked at her.

"He loves that old sweater, right?" Lucy said.

Bradley nodded.

"And we put the sweater on the leprechaun, right?" Lucy said.

"Yup," Bradley said.

"Well, Pal is a hound dog. Detectives use hound dogs to find missing people. So maybe Pal's nose can lead us to the sweater. And then we'll have the leprechaun!"

"Great idea, Lucy!" Bradley said. "And if we find our leprechaun, the other two will probably be with it!"

Bradley put his face under the bed again. "Pal, want to go for a walk?"

Pal wriggled out from under the bed. "Woof!" he said.

9
Sniffing for the Sweater

Bradley snapped on Pal's leash. He held the sweater sleeves under the dog's nose. "Find the sweater, Pal!" Bradley said.

The basset hound led the four kids down the stairs and onto the porch. He sniffed the porch floor.

"That's where we left the leprechaun," Brian said.

Pal tugged on his leash and the kids followed. They all cut through the school grounds to Main Street. Soon they were headed down Bridge Lane.

"He must be taking us back to the O'Learys' house," Nate said.

At the big blue house, Pal went straight to the red wagon. He sniffed it all over.

Just then the front door opened. Ben and Ralphie came out. "What's going on?" Ben asked.

"Pal is helping us find our leprechaun," Bradley said. "He led us here."

"He knows you put it in your wagon," Lucy said.

"He's right," Ralphie said.

"Can you let Pal sniff Lucky's gym clothes?" Bradley asked.

Ralphie giggled. "Sure, but they're pretty stinky," he said. "Come on in."

Pal and the four kids followed Ben and Ralphie inside. A bunch of redheaded kids were playing hide-and-seek. The fairy-princess leprechaun stood in a corner.

"Lucky's room is down the hall," Ben

said, leading the way. The bedroom was messy, but the bed was made.

Pal went right to a closet door. He sniffed and barked and scratched at the door.

Ben opened the closet door. The floor was covered with gym clothes. "This is where we hid them," Ralphie said.

"So somebody snuck in here and stole them," Nate said. "I wonder who."

"Do you keep your front door locked?" Bradley asked the two brothers.

Ben and Ralphie shrugged. "Mom takes care of that," Ben answered. "I guess she locks it at night. But during the day, she leaves it unlocked."

Pal left the closet and headed through the bedroom door. His leash trailed behind him.

The six kids followed.

Outside, Pal bolted for an old car sitting in the driveway. He put his front paws on the car door and started barking.

"Maybe the leprechauns are in the car!" Nate said.

"That's Lucky's car, and we already looked," Ben said. He opened the car door. Pal jumped inside. He sniffed all the seats. He found a French fry and gobbled it up. Then he barked.

"Maybe Pal thinks we're looking for Lucky," Lucy said.

Bradley pulled Pal away from the car. He let him sniff the sweater sleeves again. "Find the sweater," he told his dog. "We already know where Lucky is."

"Yeah, he's in jail," Ben said. "And it's our fault!"

Pal sat on the driveway. He looked at the kids. He looked at the car. Then he went to sleep.

10
Pal's
Nose
Knows

Bradley checked his watch. "Let's go home and eat," he said. "Then we can decide what to do next."

The kids woke up Pal. They all hiked back along Bridge Lane. When they got home, there was no car in the driveway. "Mom's still not home," Brian said.

"She left sandwiches," Bradley said.

Inside, the kids lined up at the sink and washed their hands. Pal crawled under the table to wait for crumbs.

Bradley pulled a plate of sandwiches from the fridge. Brian got out milk and glasses for everyone.

"We have tuna, peanut butter and jelly, and egg salad," Bradley said.

"Tuna!" Brian yelled.

"Egg salad!" Lucy said.

Bradley and Nate both had PB&J.

Bradley thought about Lucky and Officer Fallon. He still wondered who had told Officer Fallon that Lucky was the thief.

"We have to talk to Lucky," Bradley said.

"Why?" his brother asked.

"He might know who told Officer Fallon to arrest him," Bradley answered.

"But Lucky's in jail," Brian said.

"So we can ask Officer Fallon to let us see him," Nate said. "They let prisoners have visitors."

"How do you know?" Lucy asked.

Nate grinned. He had a milk mustache. "I saw it on TV," he said.

Ten minutes later, the kids walked up the steps of the police station. Pal pulled on his leash.

The police station was warm and quiet. A radiator hissed. A clock ticked.

"It's creepy in here," Nate whispered.

"Just be glad you're not Lucky," Lucy said. "He's in a jail cell!"

"Yuck," Brian said. "I heard they sleep on cement beds! With spiders and rats!"

"And all they feed you is bread and water!" Nate said.

"You guys watch too much TV," Lucy said.

Just then the door opened. Ben and Ralphie walked in.

"Hey, what're you guys doing here?" Ben asked.

"We came to see your brother," Bradley said.

"We did, too," Ralphie said. "We brought him some cookies." He held up a lumpy bag.

Ben looked around. "Where's his cell?" he asked.

"I think it's downstairs," Brian said.

"There's Officer Fallon's office," Bradley said. "Come on."

A small sign hung from Officer Fallon's doorknob.

It said: GONE TO LUNCH.

"It's almost one o'clock," Bradley said. "He should be back soon. Let's wait."

The six kids sat on a long bench under the clock. Ralphie held the lumpy bag on his lap. Bradley could smell the cookies. He wondered what kind they were.

Pal was sniffing the floor. Suddenly

he raced to a closed door. He began whimpering.

Bradley followed Pal. "What's the matter, boy?" he asked.

Pal's tail was going crazy. He let out a low growl. He put his front paws on the door.

Bradley opened the door. The room was dark. He found a wall switch, and a light came on.

Bradley saw mops and pails and other cleaning supplies. Against the back wall stood a huge old desk. It was partly covered with a sheet. A dusty computer sat on the desk. Spiderwebs made it look creepy. In a corner stood a tall trash barrel.

Then Bradley saw something else.

"Guys," he whispered. "Guess what Pal found?"

The five other kids hurried over to Bradley and Pal.

"Look," Bradley said. He pointed inside the room.

On a table stood three leprechauns. One had floppy ears and a doggy nose and wore part of an old sweater.

Pal leaped into the room and licked his sweater.

11
Why Is
Lucky
Laughing?

"You're awesome, Pal!" Nate said.

"Let's give these to Officer Fallon!" Ben said.

"And get Lucky out of jail!" Ralphie added.

"Wait a second," Bradley said. "Let me think."

A minute passed.

"He's thinking," Brian said.

Nate giggled.

"Something is wrong here," Bradley

said finally. "Don't you guys wonder how the leprechauns got from Lucky's closet to this storage room?"

"Maybe one of the cops found them and stuck them in here," Ben said.

"Found them where?" Ralphie said. "They never came inside to look in Lucky's closet."

"Besides, if a cop found the leprechauns, he'd have told Officer Fallon," Bradley said. "And he would have returned our leprechaun to us."

"And he wouldn't keep Lucky locked up," Ralphie said.

"You're right, Bradley," Lucy said. "Something weird is going on."

Just then they heard someone laugh.

Bradley turned around. "That came from Officer Fallon's office," he said.

Bradley thought for another minute. He tiptoed over to Officer Fallon's door. The others followed.

Six pairs of ears listened at the door.

"Your move, Officer Fallon," someone said on the other side of the door.

"That's Lucky's voice!" Ben whispered.

Very gently, Bradley turned the knob. He opened the door a few inches.

Officer Fallon was sitting at his desk. Lucky sat opposite him. They were eating burgers and playing chess.

Both had big smiles on their faces.

I thought Lucky was in jail, Bradley said to himself. He heard Ralphie and Ben take in deep breaths.

"How'd you happen to find the three leprechauns in your closet?" Officer Fallon asked Lucky.

"My mom saw Ben and Ralphie come in with the leprechauns," Lucky said. "She heard them say they were going to blame me for it. So Mom and I decided to teach those two a lesson.

That's why we brought the leprechauns here to you."

Officer Fallon laughed. "Those poor kids," he said. "They think I really arrested you. When do you want to go back home?"

"Mom says I should come back today," Lucky said. "I'll take the leprechauns with me and return them." He moved a chess piece. "But first I have to beat you at this game!"

The kids backed away from the

office door. "Did you hear that?" Ben asked. "Lucky and Officer Fallon are playing a trick on us! Lucky's not in jail at all!"

"And our mom knew about it, too!" Ralphie said.

Then he and Ben looked at each other. "I guess we deserved this," Ben said. "We started the whole thing."

"So what do we do now?" Ralphie asked.

"I have an idea," Nate said.

12
Leaping
Leprechauns

Nate led the kids into the room where the leprechauns stood on the table.

"What's your idea?" Bradley asked.

"Lucky and Officer Fallon think the leprechauns are in this room, right?" Nate said.

"Yeah, and in a few minutes, Lucky's gonna come and get them to take home again," Ralphie said.

"Only they aren't gonna be here," Nate said.

"They aren't? Where will they be?" Ben asked.

Nate grinned. "We'll hide the leprechauns again. Then, when Lucky comes to get them, they'll be gone!"

He yanked the lid off the trash barrel. There were some old newspapers in the bottom. Nate carefully lowered the leprechauns onto the papers. Then he put the lid back on.

"But what happens if someone empties the trash?" Lucy asked.

Nate shook his head. "It's Saturday," he said. "No one will look in here till Monday."

"I can't wait to see Lucky's face when he opens this door!" Ralphie crowed.

Bradley tiptoed back to Officer Fallon's office door. He peeked inside. Then he came back to the others. "I think they're finishing the game," he whispered.

"We have to hide!" Ben said. He peered around the dusty room. He pointed to the covered desk. "We can hide behind that."

They all crawled behind the desk. Pal let out a woof.

"Quiet, Pal," Bradley whispered. He pulled Pal next to him.

"I forgot the light," Ben said. He went over and hit the light switch.

Now it was black in the room.

Brian giggled. "I'm afraid of the dark," he said.

"I'll protect you," Lucy said.

"I need to sneeze!" Nate said.

"Hold your nose!" Bradley said.

"Who wants a cookie?" Ralphie mumbled through a mouthful of cookies.

Just then the door opened. Officer Fallon and Lucky looked into the dark room. The kids could see them, but they couldn't see the kids.

"They're not here!" Officer Fallon

said. "I left them on this little table!"

"I don't get it," Lucky said. "How could three statues just disappear?"

Then Bradley heard a small, muffled voice. "We're in the trash can," said the voice.

Officer Fallon didn't say anything.

Lucky didn't say anything.

They just stared into the dark room.

"Please let us out of the trash can," said the small voice. "I can hardly breathe in here!"

Officer Fallon and Lucky stepped into the room. Lucky pulled the lid off the trash can. They both peered inside.

"Well, I'll be a donkey's grandpa!" Officer Fallon said. "There they are!"

One by one, Lucky lifted the three leprechauns out of the barrel. "Can you really talk?" he said to the statues.

Behind him, six kids burst into laughter.

13
Leprechauns
Rule!

The next day was St. Patrick's Day. It was a cool, sunny morning. Bradley and Brian carried their leprechaun to the town hall lawn. Pal walked along next to them. Lucy and Nate were waiting.

"There must be a million leprechauns here!" Nate said.

The kids looked around. Leprechauns stood everywhere. They had all started out looking exactly the same. Now they were all different.

The leprechauns were all dressed or decorated or painted. There were rock stars, sports figures, and nurses. Bradley saw a Mickey Mouse and an Elvis. He waved to Josephine and her fairy princess. He saw Officer Fallon holding the police leprechaun.

Ben and Ralphie came over to say hi.

"What's yours supposed to be, anyway?" Ralphie asked. "A giant hamster?"

"It's our dog, Pal," Bradley explained.

"I wonder who will win first prize," Ralphie said.

Brian grinned. "Us," he said. "We have the only talking leprechaun."

They all laughed. "At least Lucky and Officer Fallon were cool about getting busted like that," Ralphie said. "They admitted how they tricked us."

"Which one of you guys did that funny voice yesterday?" Bradley asked.

"Not me!" Ben and Ralphie said at the same time.

"We had cookies in our mouths!" Ralphie said.

"It wasn't me, either," Nate said. "I was trying not to sneeze."

"I certainly didn't do it," Lucy said. She looked at Bradley and Brian. "I thought it was one of you two."

Brian shook his head. "Not guilty," he said. "And it wasn't Bradley, either. He was squished right next to me."

"So who was it?" Nate asked. "We all heard somebody say, 'Please let us out of the trash can,' right?"

"Gee, maybe it *was* your leprechaun," Ben said. He put his hand on the leprechaun dressed as Pal.

The six kids stared at the statue.

Just then the mayor of Green Lawn stepped out of the town hall. The crowd cheered and the mayor waved. He walked among the leprechauns, chatting with people and patting kids on the head. His assistant walked with him, taking notes on a clipboard.

The mayor stopped in front of the leprechaun dressed as a dog.

"And what have we here?" the mayor asked. "A dog leprechaun?"

"Yes, sir," Bradley said. "It's a basset hound. It's supposed to look like our dog, Pal."

Pal woofed at the mayor.

"Oh, I see," said the mayor. "Very cute. Very clever." He whispered something to his assistant.

She scribbled a note.

The mayor walked away.

Soon the mayor had examined all the leprechauns. He and his assistant walked up the town hall steps. A microphone was waiting for him.

"Good morning, and happy St. Patrick's Day!" the mayor said. "I'm happy to see that so many of you believe in leprechauns! This is the biggest turnout I've ever seen!"

More clapping and whistling.

The mayor took the clipboard from his assistant. "It seems we have a tie this year!" he said. "We have two winners!"

Everybody looked at one another's leprechauns.

"Our first winner is Fairy-Princess Leprechaun!" he yelled. "Will its owner please come up here?"

Josephine O'Leary and her whole family ran up the steps and stood by the mayor. Ben and Ralphie carried the fairy-princess statue.

The mayor placed a big green ribbon around the leprechaun's neck.

Everybody cheered. Lucky lifted Josephine up onto his shoulders.

"And our second winner is Basset Hound Leprechaun!" the mayor went on. "Where are its owners?"

Bradley grabbed the leprechaun. He led Brian, Nate, Lucy, and Pal up to join the mayor. The mayor dropped a ribbon around the leprechaun's shoulders.

Bradley grinned and hugged his leprechaun. The crowd cheered.

Then Bradley heard a small voice in his ear. "Leprechauns rule!" it said.

Bradley stared at the leprechaun.

The leprechaun stared back.

Maybe it was the sun in his eyes, but Bradley could have sworn the leprechaun was winking.

Track down all these books for a little mystery in your life!

A to Z Mysteries®
by Ron Roy

Calendar Mysteries
by Ron Roy

Capital Mysteries
by Ron Roy

Marion Dane Bauer
The Blue Ghost
The Green Ghost
The Red Ghost
The Secret of the Painted House

Polly Berrien Berends
The Case of the Elevator Duck

Éric Sanvoisin
The Ink Drinker

George Edward Stanley
Ghost Horse

How many of KC and Marshall's adventures have you read?

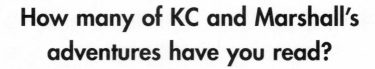

Capital Mysteries

www.randomhouse.com/kids/capitalmysteries

2/10